WELCOME
TO
SUNNYDALE

Enjoy Your Stay!

POPULATION 38,500   ESTABLISHED 1909

BRONZE

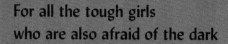
**For all the tough girls
who are also afraid of the dark**

Library of Congress Cataloging in Publication Number:
2017961230
ISBN: 978-1-68369-071-9
Printed in China
Typeset in Miller and Gill Sans

Story and text by Jason Rekulak
Designed by Doogie Horner
Production management by John J. McGurk

Special thanks to Joss Whedon, Carol Roeder, Nicole Spiegel,
Julie Scott, and Rebecca Gyllenhaal

Quirk Books
215 Church Street
Philadelphia, PA 19106
quirkbooks.com

10 9 8 7 6 5 4 3 2 1

Buffy
the vampire slayer

Based on the series created by Joss Whedon

Illustrated by Kim Smith

QUIRK BOOKS
PHILADELPHIA

It's not easy being a vampire slayer.

Everywhere I go, vampires hide in the shadows, waiting to attack.

Fortunately, I've learned how to fight back!

My name is Buffy Summers, and I hunt vampires.

But here's a secret nobody knows: I wasn't always this tough.

When I was eight years old,
I was afraid of the dark.

And I knew there was
a MONSTER in my closet!

I could hear it making noises.

SNIFF SCRATCH BUMP THUMP!

So I asked my friends Willow and Xander to sleep over.

I'm Willow.

And I'm Xander.

It's pronounced
Zander.

We had a great time together.

We played games,

ate popcorn,

made pillow forts,

and listened to music.

And at the end of the night, Mom tucked
us into our beds.

And turned off the light.

And sure enough, the noises started again.

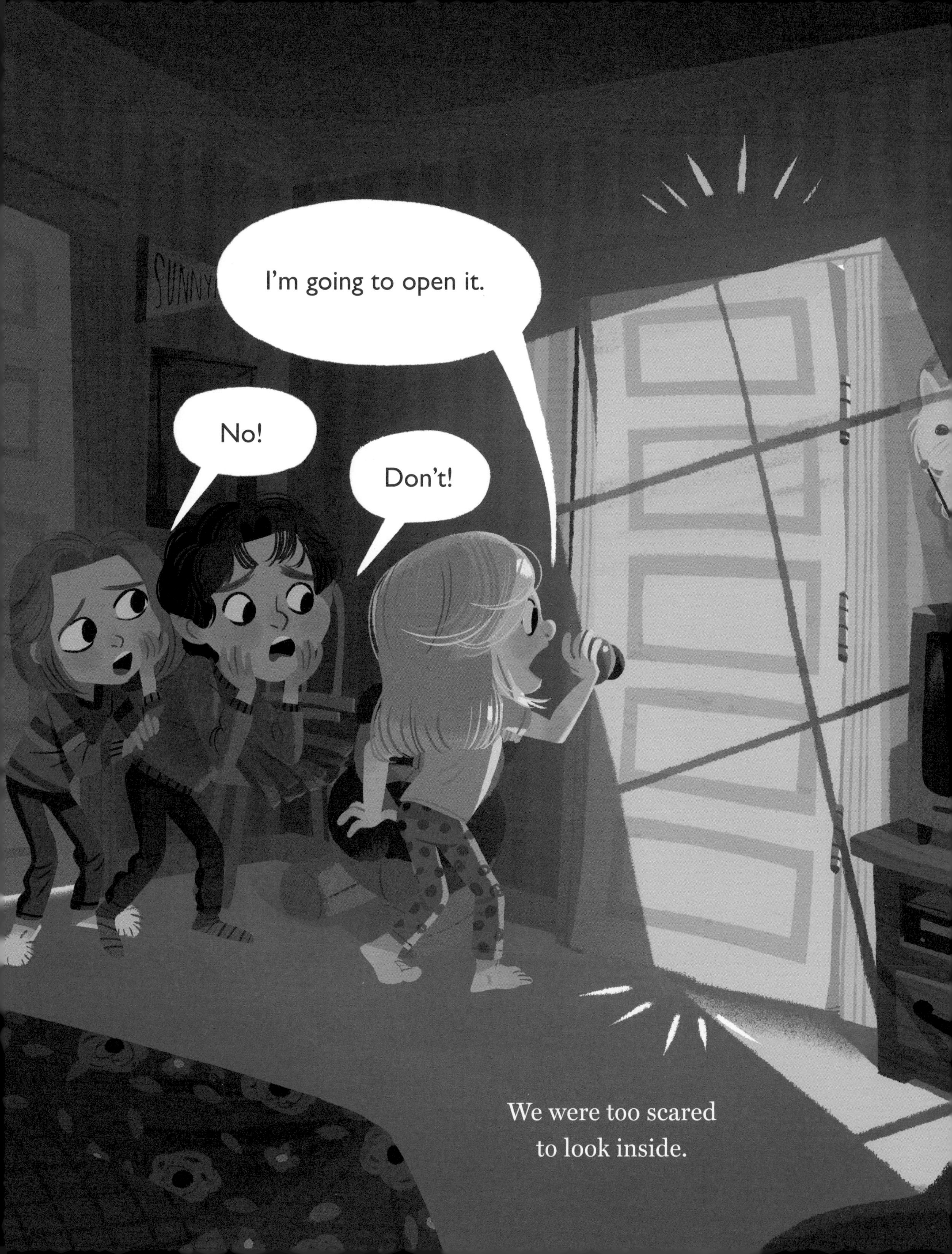

We were too scared
to look inside.

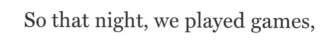

So that night, we played games,

ate popcorn,

made pillow forts,

and listened to music.

But it wasn't the same.
We were all pretty nervous.

At the end of the night,
Mom turned off the light.

And soon the noises started again.

SNIFF SCRATCH!

BUMP THUMP!

I got up to open the door. And inside the closet, we saw . . .

Together we stepped into the darkness.

Well, I felt terrible. My closet was very small and uncomfortable.
It's no wonder the monsters were so noisy.

Or some tissues?

Can I bring you a blanket?

That night, our little slumber party had a few new guests.

We played games, ate popcorn, made pillow forts, and listened to music.

It was the best sleepover ever . . .

Until Mom came to check on us.

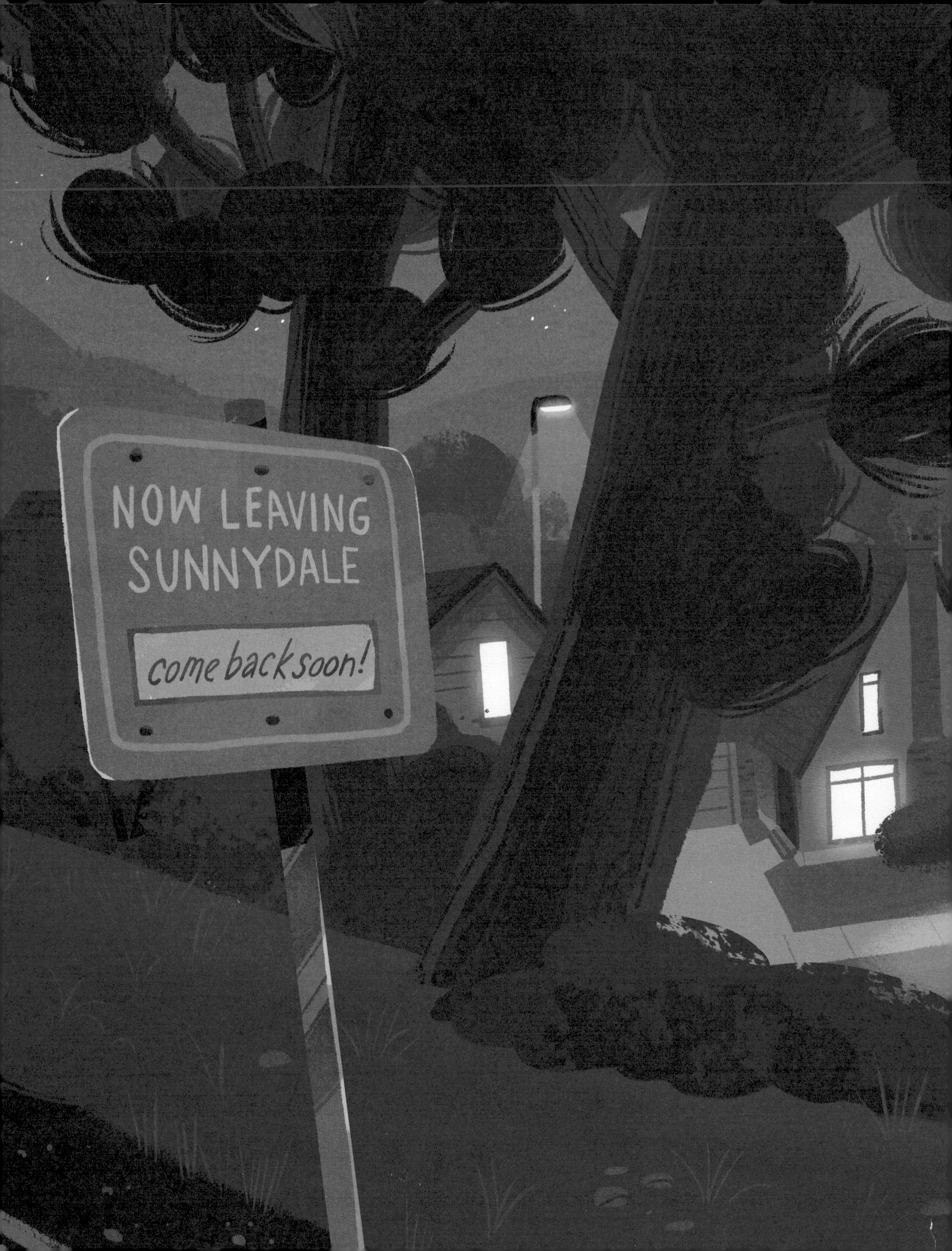
NOW LEAVING
SUNNYDALE
come back soon!